ALLISTER CROMLEY'S
FAIRWEATHER BELLE
(Bedtime Stories For Grownups To Tell)

Thank you to all who contributed their talents and made this book possible.

⊖ **Artwork** (in order of appearance)

Melissa McMillan
Jim Senti
Dave Droxler
Annie Peters
Dallah Cesen
emme b
Kelly Martinez
Kristian Michael Hickman
Lark O Arrowood
Marie Elena O'Brien
Angelica Joy Miskanin
A.D. Peters
Aaron Martinez

⊖ **Editor**
Amanda B. Gillooly

⊖ **Cover Art**
Dave Droxler

⊖ **Cover & Book Design**
Ruth Gamble & Shane Portman

⊖ **Title Font & Page Font**
Captain's Table
by Roulette Studios
&
Ogdred Weary
by nonDairy Publishing

And a special thank you to my sisters who were the first (and sometimes reluctant) audience for the Allister stories when we were kids. And to Mike Balzer who said, "You know what you should call your Allister Cromley stories? The Fairweather Belle."

ISBN-10: 0615632637
ISBN-13: 978-0615632636 (S. Portman)

The stories that follow are the first in a collection of tall tales about a malleable man. And there is a hope sewn into the title- that the passages may be read aloud from person to person.

In all the confusion of today, it's becoming increasingly hard to find something sturdy to hold onto; something other than cynicism.

And, when I was a child, I remember feeling much like I do now- that the world is full of unanswered questions. But back then, when I was tucked in tight and read bedtime stories, I felt safe and even excited about all the questions that lay in the dark.

It was a sweet and simple magic that I think we can find again.

TO BEGIN. A PROLOGUE.

It has often been said that the easiest way to write is to use your own personal experiences. I beg to differ. For me, it has always been easiest to write about Allister Cromley. And it's not that I do not find my own life interesting. It's just that I am currently involved in it and have been for some time now. Writing down my life, while in the process of also living it, would be like living twice—but only getting the actual feeling of it once.

Now, Allister and I have long been friends and I would have chronicled his life much sooner, but he made me promise to wait. You see, Allister had bigger plans that would begin only after he passed on. Each night, while we slept peacefully, he wanted to send each and every subconscious their very own personalized three-hour Allister Cromley biopic, hand-crafted to fit each individual's particular tastes. But, my fear is that he underestimated the number of people in this world.

Some day, my friends. Some day.

Until then, I shall just have to depend on spreading the word to you and you spreading it to whomever you will until we have reached the far corners of the world (where, at one time, Allister owned and operated a small windmill).

A PIGEON

ow, many people find pigeons to be an animal made of exclusively repulsive and asinine parts. In Allister's time, too, many referred to the pigeon as the "rat of the skies." And perhaps Allister would have felt the same way if he had not met one particular pigeon whilst sitting on a bench along a gravely path in a park not too far from where you may now live.

The pigeon strolled up to Allister's feet in that way pigeons so often do—that head-bobbing stumble that looks as if the pigeon only vaguely understands how to use its feet.

The pigeon promptly began to peck at Allister's boots.

And perhaps one could chalk this up to being a simple error, that the pigeon mistook the boot for bread (they were both brown after all). But, the pigeon was stubborn. And it was only when the stubbornness stretched and the pecking fervor increased, as if the pigeon believed that the harder it pecked the more likely the boot would turn to bread, that Allister finally felt compelled to give the pigeon a polite shove with his foot.

The bird's body felt like a sack—a tiny sack of tiny bird bones (if one were to attempt a simultaneous description of both a figurative and literal nature). The bird hobbled back a

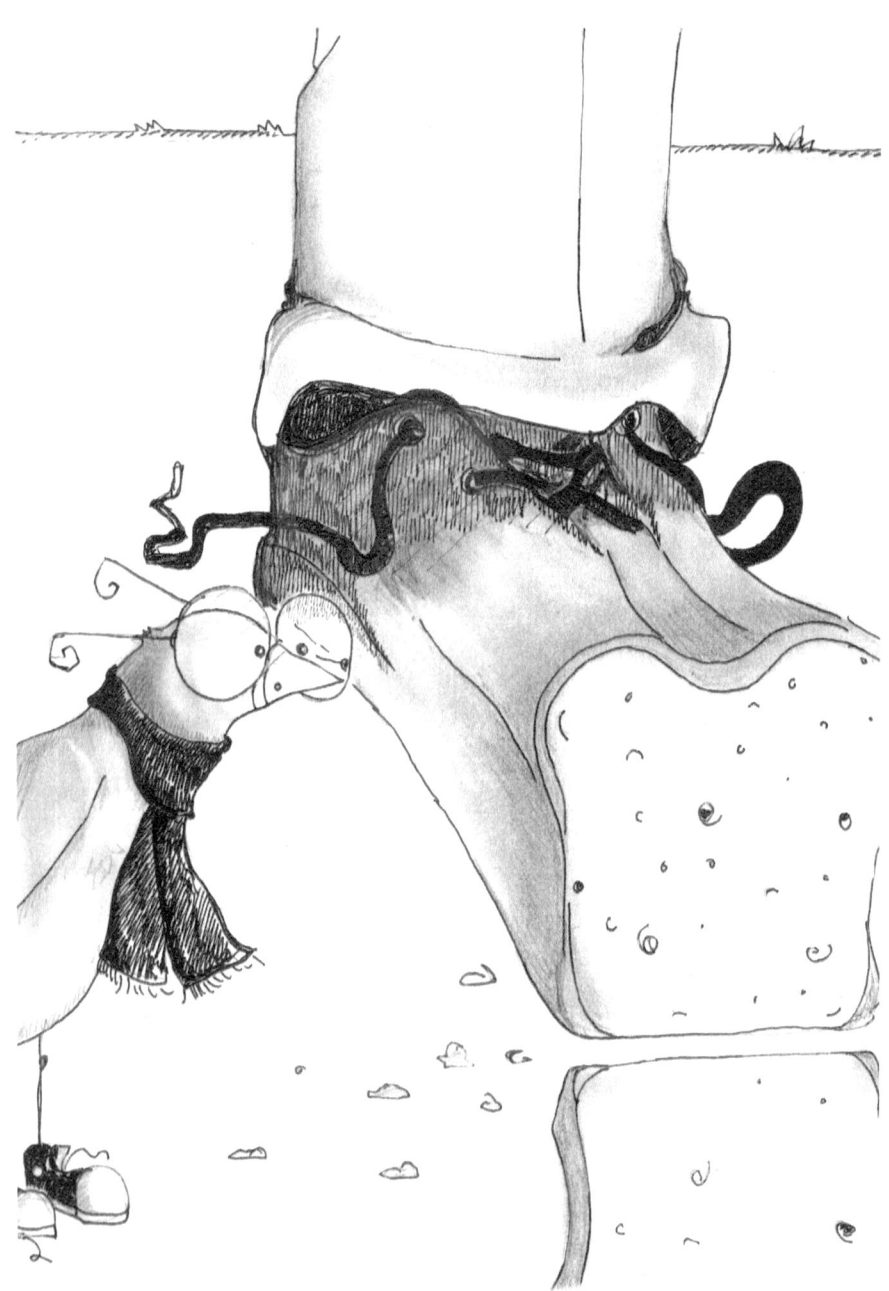

few steps seemingly unaware of the reason for the hobbling. But, whence the idea that the bread had pushed sunk into the bird's brain, it raised its head and a pigeon eye met Allister's human eye. And there they stood, locked together.

Allister felt the pigeon's grey pear body heave and contract as if it breathed from its eye. And Allister felt the surprise of the pigeon, understood the loss of innocence that came from the discovery of a world where bread becomes a kicking boot.

The pigeon was suddenly helpless and Allister tried to send the connection from his human eye to the pigeon eye, tried to heave and contract his own body so that the pigeon understood that the world was not the way he thought it would be either; that surprises of the frightening variety were not exclusive to pigeons.

But, the pigeon just stood there. Not a single twitch. Not a single head bob. And Allister wondered if the pigeon would simply die right then. Had its world disappeared? Where do you go and what do you eat when bread fights back? Allister thought that, if he were the reason for this pigeon's most depressing end, he would most certainly have to take his own life. The feelings were that severe. The mourning was palpable. Anguish became audible. The air smelled of despair. Sadness could be tasted in all things.

And at the brink of that uncompromising pain—when the pigeon's head should have simply bent forward and fallen

to the ground, followed soon after by its grey pear body—
something most surprising happened.

The pigeon's head did not fall.

Instead, it bobbed. And kept bobbing. Its feet kicked
in that vague malaise of a walk and, when its head did finally
bend, it seemed to be done in answer to Allister's concern
over what the pigeon would now eat. And Allister watched,
for the remaining moments of the day, as the pigeon
stumbled clumsily down the path and pecked with satisfaction
at a wide selection of stones and gravel.

A BROKEN VASE

Allister never knew when he was born. To punish him for breaking a vase, his parents never told him the date. So, every year, Allister would throw a party on Mondays, Wednesdays and Fridays with the hope that sooner or later his party would land on his actual birthday.

And, then, perhaps he would hear that divine whisper in his ear. "Psst Allister. Happy Birthday, son."

But, years passed and Allister aged. I could no longer even count the number of "birthday" parties I had attended in Allister's honor. And, as the years passed, less and less happened at these parties. You could only eat cake and ice cream for so long. Pin the tail on the donkey wore thin with a regiment of playing three days a week. People no longer knew what to get him. No one had that piece of information he was looking for. We did not even know how many candles to put on the cake. It was awkward. Sad...and awkward.

He cursed himself daily for the reckless destruction of that vase so long ago. He had tried to glue it back together. But, there were holes where the fall had pulverized the ceramic to dust. His parents shook their heads. It was not enough. That vase was special. Not knowing where to turn and badly wanting a birthday, he went to the kitchen cabinet and broke the extra set of saucers until they fit into the holes of the ramshackle vase.

With the glue drying, Allister looked on with a sense of pride. He had not thought about the anger his parents would have when they set eyes on his repairs and realized that they, now, had only one set of saucers. Where would they put their extra teacups? With his parents' anger over their saucers came the realization that he could not possibly put anything back the way it once was.

Instead, year after year, Allister tried to replace the memory of his parents' broken vase with a brand new one, until his house became a collection of vases. Hundreds of vases. Some placed strategically and some stacked carelessly atop other vases. But, none of them could take the place of that broken one. And, at the end of the year, Allister would know for sure he was another year older but, how old, he could not tell.

Allister eventually told us not to get him any presents (although, truthfully, most of us had already stopped long ago). He just wanted our company on those Mondays, Wednesdays and Fridays. Cake and ice cream had been replaced by prune juice and multi-vitamins. Pin the tail on the donkey became pinochle. He had given up ever knowing his age when he heard the whisper.

He rose from his wicker lawn chair with a giggle. We had thought he had finally gone mad in his old age. He gripped his cane and hobbled, as lively as I had ever seen him hobble, into the house. There was a silence. A howl of laughter. And then, the audible barrage of ceramic breaking as Allister laid waste to hundreds of vases with his cane.

Hours later, he appeared in the doorway and hobbled back to us covered in ceramic dust and sweat, but a smile pulled across his face. We looked at him, stunned as deer. He sat down slowly in his wicker chair, set his cane down beside him with utmost care, and folded his hands in his lap before saying, "I heard it."

Not knowing what to do in that situation—when a good friend might possibly have become a psychopath right in front of your eyes and with the weapon he used to bash all his inner demons resting next to him—I simply asked, "How old are you?" He looked at me, grinned, and said:

"They said it does not matter."

TY COBB

Allister always admired many people. But, few could rival the admiration that Allister felt for Ty Cobb, the Detroit Tigers' belligerent outfielder. The following correspondence was found in a small trunk of letters buried in the ground beneath a larger trunk of letters.

The initial letter was written when Allister was in grade school. And it reads as follows:

Dear Mr. Cobb,

My name is Allister. Please excuse eny grammur with spilling errors as I am olny in grade school and you are reelly good at baseball. Also you are my faverite player and I think you are reelly good at it. I write to you to tell you that and also because a friend of mine is named Tommy he said you were meen. I told him you were not meen and he said you were meen again. You are my hero Mr. Cobb and I hope you are not meen. Keep playing good baseball forever.

Sinsurly,
Allister Cromley

Months passed without a response. Little Allister grew three inches and disheartened during the long wait. A year and more passed with more disheartening and more inches.

Dear Mr. Cobb
   My name is Allister,
Please excuse eny grammur
with spilling errors as I am
olny in grade school and you
are reelly good at baseball.
   Also

Finally, Allister reached 5 feet and 9 inches with no hope left in his heart. That, of course, was precisely the time when the letter arrived. The envelope was yellowed. Allister removed the letter inside and it read as follows:

Dear Allister,

Son, I do appreciate your patronage on my behalf. And I will say that I mean only so much disrespect toward other ballplayers. I do not necessarily want to come off as a mean old son of a bitch. But, I will tell you this: If you, young Allister, were a second baseman and you had the unfortunate circumstance of playing for the team opposing my team, I would most certainly sink my spikes into your shins. I know that you are only a young boy in grade school. But, do not be mistaken. I would still sharpen my cleats to their most heinous points for the game. Thank you again for your nice letter. It brought a smile to my face.

Sincerely,
Ty Cobb

PS Please have your mother read this letter first, as I am not sure if someone your age should be reading a phrase like 'son of a bitch'.

SOFTLY SPOKEN

Allister rarely spoke above a whisper. His vocal chords were sensitive. Allister attributed this to a childhood habit of drinking water from a rusty pail, although there is no medical evidence to support this theory.

In fact, some circles believe the contrary—that the increase in rust would thereby increase his iron intake, thus making him healthier. It should be noted that this theory also lacks proper medical evidence.

Theories aside, though eloquent, Allister was most certainly quiet. This quite often was mistaken for sheepishness or shyness (previously thought to be one and the same). Such was not the case. Though quiet, Allister erupted in excitement. Or, was it giddiness? He would be the first to admit that he did not always know how to share this with anyone—how he loved to frolic in the pauses, painting pictures, and following imaginary lines-like sunshine squirting from a fellow's nose. His world was at once ours and at once only his.

Understandably, the quiet made some uncomfortable. More than once (let's say 68 times) the host of a party would reach toward Allister in that way you would find a shepherd reaching for a baby lamb bleating and mangled by a wolf. But, Allister was not bleating. He was not mangled by a wolf. He was not a baby lamb and he wished not to be treated so.

It was an argument that his silence defeated his wishes and made him look devastatingly sad. But, that discrepancy only occurred if you paid attention solely to the lack of Allister's voice and not to the corners of his mouth.

Because, if you had been paying attention to those corners, you would have noticed an ever so slightly upward point from both sides making the slightest of smirks.

Whilst others dreaded the silence, Allister sculpted the pauses into structures of such majesty that they could only exist in his quiet. He would, of course, speak when he felt the drip of conversation in his mouth. But, not unless needed. Too much was to be done in the quiet. The table was playing a most disadvantaged game of tag with the chairs. The salt and pepper shakers were discussing Voltaire in that hearty manner of spices.

And when the music would begin and the party would "finally start," as some would say, and all collected on the dance floor, waving Allister to join them, he often times was happier where he was. After all, there was a symphony being conducted in the quiet. And light was bouncing and giggling off of the chandelier crystals.

FROM A TRENCH NEAR AND FAR AWAY

Allister, like so many, found himself crouched deep inside the narrow trenches carved throughout Western Europe in the autumn of 1917. Dirty, hungry and defeated (though history books would later claim him the victor), Allister lived in the Earth's scars. There was the music of rifles punctuated by the booming bass of far away cannons. And there was the eerie silence that followed. There was the nervous crossing of fingers and the whistle blowing of a general and the mad crossing through the pockmarks of No Man's Land.

In letters found later, Allister wrote of the awkward awareness that off in the distance lay more scars and that when rifles were fired, they were not shot into darkness but beyond the darkness and into men of a different cause. It was a duality that Allister lived with from day to day (though it seemed the sun never rose). In civilian life, he would never have thought about killing another man. But in battle, Allister found the belief that the bullet he fired could take down the man who would tip the balance and give them the edge and win the battle and perhaps end the war. It was not the death of the man that Allister wanted, but the end of the war.

Tension seemed to connect moments of extreme pain with unexpected bursts of laughter. In the tension, Allister felt the scars narrowing, closing, as if the Earth was attempting to heal itself. And it was in those moments, between pain and

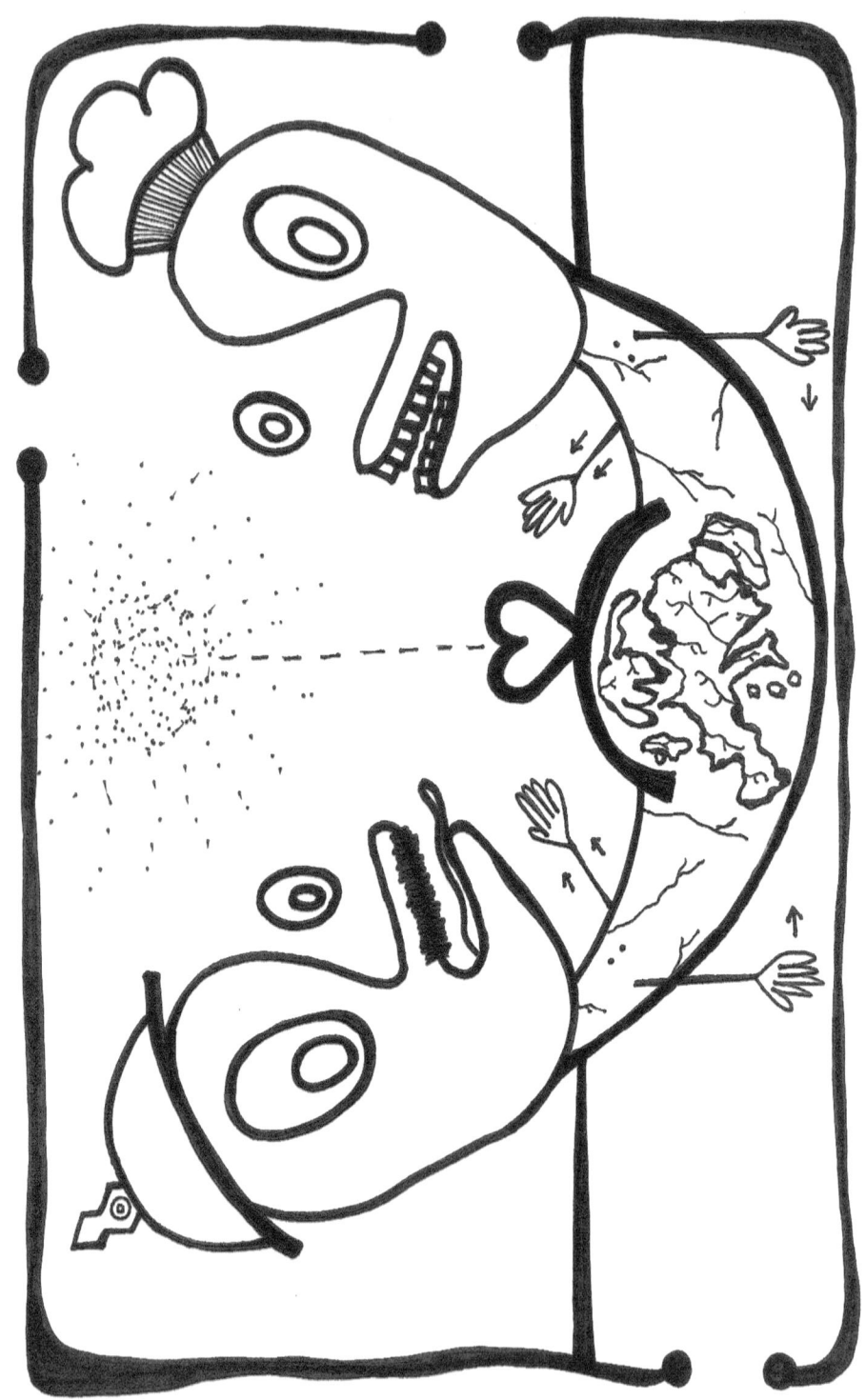

joy, that Allister found time to remember that this was not all there was—that there was somewhere to go home to. And those memories were what drove Allister to write his letters, though he did not write home.

He wrote of loss and gain and the absurdity of all the different men in his regiment; men of different form and background and shape and size and goals and occupation; attempting to look the same in the same uniform. He wrote of how he mused on creating regiments based on civilian job, where all bakers would man the artillery, for instance, in their aprons and white floppy hats. He confessed that, in moments of heavy fire, he often found himself chuckling at the idea of firing only at the pointed spikes of the enemy's helmets, whilst the enemy sent machine gun fire clipping the sides of his own pan-shaped helmet and spun it in circles atop his head. A mad carnival of tipping points and spinning pans.

When finished, he would fold the letter carefully and address it to "A Friend." In later letters, he would shorten the address to just "Friend." He would place the letter in his pocket to rest until he found himself furiously charging through the middle of No Man's Land. There, he would find a long-discarded helmet of the pointed variety, dimpled and dented in a pattern so original that it could only have been made during battle. And he would lay the letter carefully underneath the helmet. It was there that his pen pal and rival first discovered it, surely whilst ducking from fire and, just as surely, from fire that Allister was contributing.

His pen pal read the note and left a reply to be found on Allister's company's next charge. In it, he agreed about the silliness of carpenter, lawyer, and baker attempting to dress alike. He added that, amidst heavy fire, he thought not of helmets, but mused on the idea of both sides rising above the trenches, forming kick lines, and punting mortars and bombs and grenades back and forth and into the air, exploding in a display of fireworks, the likes of which had never been seen before.

Their letters spanned the length of the campaign, touching on topics as simple as hobbies and as complex as who was right and who was wrong and whether it mattered much anymore. On life and death and family and friends. On boredom and confusion. Allister knew of his friend's friends and his friend knew of Allister's friends and, when one of them would fall, they would promise the other to remember their name and character, "For someone always should." And, though pictures were never sent and the issue was never addressed, Allister was sure that his friend also had a mustache.

Living in their scars, they both felt them closing in. They mused on how the Earth in front of them both was brown, how blood dries brown, how we continue to find ourselves carving through the blood of our ancestors killed long ago. How small lessons were learned from each battle, but larger ones were left to be discovered. They wrote of the ratio of questions to answers and whether that had any correlation with the ratio of war to peace.

And, when finished writing, they carefully folded their notes, loaded their weapons, fixed their bayonets, crossed their fingers, waited for the whistle, and charged into the darkness.

WINSTON CHURCHILL

Though Allister never smoked cigarettes; he did, on occasion, smoke cigars. That occasion would arrive any time Allister found himself with Winston Churchill. This, of course, would not be the Winston Churchill you think of—if, indeed, you think of Winston Churchill. No, this was before Winston Churchill was Winston Churchill. Or, at least, before Winston Churchill knew he was Winston Churchill. Or, rather, before Winston Churchill knew he was the Winston Churchill that we remember.

There were similarities, to be sure. Both smoked cigars. Both had eyes, noses, hands, feet, shoulders, hips. Both walked behind the lead of a polished cane. And neither Winston could be remembered for selling themselves short in conversation. In fact, it was reasonable and valid and vice versa to say that, on many occasions, both Winstons sold themselves far too long.

But there were differences, to be just as sure. For, Allister's Winston tended to wear high heels, tended to redden his lips, and tended to prefer the comfort of a skirt to the comfort of pants. As to why that was, one found it hard to question Winston. One found one's self, as Allister found himself, sitting across from Winston—drawn in by the largeness, by the character, by the person. And, in lieu of questions, Allister found himself imitating Winston—who inhaled so deeply until all that was once cigar became but ash.

And, in the most proper and polite manner, Winston would lower what was once cigar and tap from its nubby butt.

On command, the ash would rain down over the ashtray and collect into a puddle of itself. And Winston would look down with his painted eyes and make the slightest noise of surprise to insinuate that he had not expected that.

And Allister always smiled. For, when smoking cigars, the fall of ash should come as no surprise. Winston would smile back at Allister. And, with the flick of two pudged fingers, Winston would swallow the cigar nub as if it were a candy—as if that were normal. And, if Allister's attempts at mimicking Winston were not identical, they were at least dramatic.

Instead of the sweet simplicity of Winston's swallowing a cigar nub like candy, there came Allister's gagging and almost-suffocating. And that would leave Allister staring forward with bloodshot eyes—stunned, surprised, and speechless. And Winston would smile—for Allister's surprise, too, should have come as no surprise.

And, perhaps, Winston would redden his lips. Or, perhaps, he would be happy with how red his lips already were. And they would sit and smile. And Allister never knew if Winston would wonder. But, Allister would. He would wonder the whole walk home, in fact—while Winston wrote with the softened nub of lipstick on bridges and sculptures and park benches and lamp posts with lanterns slowly dimming, the simple (and later, the somewhat, but not entirely misleading) claim:

Winston Churchill was here.

SUBTLE ANARCHY

In days when anarchists hurled homemade bombs at politicians, Allister lived a more subtle life of anarchy. That is to say if he had passed a sign that said 'Stop,' he would have written underneath, 'Or go.'

Hours were spent in single library sections, transplanting Poe and Shelley to the non-fiction and Webster's Dictionary to the fiction section. And those, of course, would not rest in the pleasance of alphabetical order. Oh, no. With Allister's assistance, Poe would nestle beside Defoe and they would be sandwiched between an atlas and an 18th century arithmetic text.

When trimming his hair, be it scalp or mustache, Allister made sure that each snip of the scissor removed a different length so that his hair remained a physical display of individuality. The disorganization was betrayed only by Allister's unforgiving part, which forced a canal of organized scalp through the left side of his masterful disarray.

Allister's speech bounced from syllable to syllable in no particular order. His tie was sometimes arranged in a bow, sometimes a Windsor, sometimes a half Windsor, sometimes a Pratt, and sometimes around his ankle.

On the Sabbath, Allister refused to rest, choosing instead to stay awake for each and every single minute of the 24 hours (sometimes taking it even further by remaining completely active, leaping the entire day, for example). And when the refusal to rest became a rule of his own, he simply changed form and refused to address any of the days of the week by name.

And though these subtle rebellions brought about the end to no regimes, destroyed no government systems be they evil or good, changed no one in particular, Allister enjoyed the simplicity of breaking form. He enjoyed reading backward and diagonal as well as forward. He loved listening through his eyes and nose and toes as well as his ears. He loved being called Allison or Dudley or Günter or Georgia or Allister. He loved drinking from bowls and eating out of cups. And this changed no overall opinion, created no bloodshed that freed us all from the restraints of bigwigs. But, from time to time, it did give Allister a giggle—a burst of spontaneity that even he had no control over.

And Allister, well, he continued to follow no rules (not even ones written by himself) until following no rules in itself became, by definition, a rule.

NEW BEGINNINGS

When Allister stepped into a train, a bus, a trolley, a ship, a submarine, a zeppelin, or an elevator he always did the same thing. His eyes searched for traces of possible friendship in all the other eyes. And he looked at hair and shoulders and height and feet. For, no matter how confident Allister was in the driver of the vehicle—or in cases such as the elevator, the man in the pillbox hat who pulled the lever and said, "Going up," or, "Going Down"—there always itched the possibility, however slight, that one could get stuck in the capsule. The train could veer off track, the zeppelin unexpectedly drop into the Alps, the submarine sink to the depths, the ship sink down on top of the submarine.

This was somewhat reality. A slight somewhat reality, to be sure. But, a somewhat reality just the same.

Allister did not revel in catastrophe. He did not choose to think that way. He would merely catch the anxious feeling midway through his scan, as if the fear of a crash were the common cold or typhus (where and when typhus was a common illness). And, immediately, Allister would prepare the only way someone could.

He would search for the sweet eyes of the one he would fall in love with, would marry and raise a family with in that train car, that deflated zeppelin.

And he would search for the patch-covered eye, pointed dark mustache, and evil glare of the man with the dark gentleman's cane who would most certainly become his arch nemesis—who would somehow find ways to prosper and abuse the rest of the population of that elevator car, that trolley.

He would search, too, for the calm, wide shoulders and the simple, honest smile of Allister's newest life-long best friend—whom he would surely have to protect from his arch-nemesis who most certainly preyed on those simple, honest souls.

And he would search for the doctor, the nurse, the farmer (cultivating corn and tomatoes from leather seats and steel bars), the philosopher, the mayor, the judge, the sheriff, the scientist, the tailor, and the man whose nervous twitch and cross-eyed stare betrayed quite clearly that he was all too eager to leap to cannibalism much earlier than necessary.

And, in one place, Allister would see the general store stocked with gum and hard candy scraped from the bottom of seats. And, in another, the restaurant where at first all would feast on leather strips and then nothing at all—everyone sitting at the long table and imagining they were eating filet mignon on imaginary plates with imaginary forks and knives. And then, perhaps, if necessary (but—and this should be stressed for the man with the twitch—only when absolutely necessary), a person.

And there were the tailor and the cobbler shops and hardware store and the office of the newspaper editor. All in that train car, that bus, that trolley, that ship, that submarine, that zeppelin, that elevator. No one understanding how or why the entrances and exits would not work and why no one had come to save them. Everyone just moving on, adapting to Allister's fantasy.

And Allister would work his way through that whole life—of love and loss and good and evil and children and grandchildren—as the train, the bus, the trolley, the ship, the submarine, the zeppelin, the elevator traveled along, carrying Allister, his new companions, and their new lives to their desired destinations. And, when the doors did open, when the ramps were let down, and people made their exits, Allister would mark them off as though they had just forfeited their place—until the doors opened and the ramps were let down for Allister, too.

And he would find himself exiting.

A FOLD

If one found Allister with his hand tucked inside his pocket, one could assume that between his fingers was the piece of paper Allister had been folding for his entire life. It had started as a single fold, the most common of folds—right through the middle—and had turned into another and another. The reason for even the first fold was lost somewhere along the way. And now the reasoning had become simply to fold. To bend the paper into itself in such a way that it was smaller and, perhaps one day, that it would disappear altogether into nothing.

Allister had always been fascinated with nothing—that something was something and nothing was nothing and in between there was no other step. Yet, the line where one leaped so completely into the other was so miniscule, so impossibly invisible to all senses that it baffled. How did something become something in the first place? From nothing? And where did something return into nothing?

Allister, at times, wondered if he had been here before. He could, for instance, sometimes picture himself near Socrates when he made the decision to peacefully swallow the hemlock—not, of course, in human form. For, that moment was for that man alone. Allister, though, could feel himself there, perhaps as a bench or some long-forgotten brick. And, without eyes to see, Allister could feel the moment the man's eyes shut. The moment Socrates decided to turn his powerful

mind off, to simply adhere to the jury, to make his thoughts—his breath disappear.

For good? For bad? He was gone.

And Allister would fold the paper in his pocket—so small already—and yet, not gone. It was still there—so tiny. In latter years, the paper was so small that one could scarcely see it on Allister's finger tip-the folds so precise, the paper compressed into itself so tightly that it still carried the weight, but lacked the size to prove it.

And, if you put this speck of seeming nothing under a microscope, you would see that it was indeed something.

In those simple folds, those compressions and creases of a single piece of paper, Allister attempted to find the place where the two met—where something faded into nothing. And he wondered if it ever did. Did Socrates disappear with his breath? Did his breath disappear at all? Was it still coasting through the breeze, whispering in listening ears? Was something, in itself, nothing? Was nothing, in itself, something?

And yet, one could—as a human—understand the birth of an idea and the loss of an idea. How it springs from nowhere, how inspiration rises not only from ashes but also from absences. And how it seemingly disappears just as quickly, only to rise again when least expected. The questions come with answers and the answers with questions. And sometimes one's contribution to a new idea is just the thought that that idea is possible. Sometimes we will see nothing more than that in our lifetime. But, isn't that something?

Allister folded so small, so tiny, that it seemed as though the piece of paper did, indeed, truly disappear into nothing. Allister could feel it on his fingertip and he would show us all. He would put his finger underneath a light so close and we would squint and look so hard that migraines were born. And we would see nothing.

But, we knew otherwise.

THE ESCALATOR

Allister remembered, with the same clarity that some remembered assassinations of world leaders or victorious battles that ended wars, the day he first saw stairs move. He stood with a crowd that gasped in unison at the new escalator inside Harrod's Department Store. That gasping easily passed the 15-minute mark. A world had been shattered. Stairs were moving. Perhaps there was a nugget of fear—that if stairs were evolving, if stairs were moving, it was only a matter of time before they straightened their form entirely, broke free from their rail-y confines, and walked upright past the human race.

Perhaps that fear, even if too small to be consciously recognized, danced in the terrified pupils of those bewildered onlookers. If all stairways evolved and walked away from their stores, how on Earth would we reach the second floor? Or the third floor? Elevators? Who would want to rely solely on those beasts?

Perhaps that illogical fear was all assumptive on Allister's part—that no one's mind jumped to such ridiculous phobia. But, this can certainly be said: After 15 minutes of gawking, not a single person set a single foot on a single traveling step. No matter how courageous one had been in some other form of life, that was too much. The crowd simultaneously turned its back on the escalator.

All that is, but one.

A young girl, perhaps 4, had slipped from the maternal grip of her mother's gloved hand and strolled to the moving beast that whirred with the mechanical growls of rotators and pinions. These did not scare her. She offered her right hand to the escalator as if it were a scared stray mutt who growled in defense but whose eyes betrayed its ferocious exterior, its need for a rub behind the ears—as if the escalator had eyes. Or ears.

And the escalator did not snap. Allister was the first to notice, turning back just in time. The escalator did not snap. The little girl set her little pointer finger to a step emerging from some deep mysterious abyss that lived in the floor. She let the gentle beast guide her hand up until it was pulled just enough to be too far and she giggled. She pulled her hand back and giggled—and simply placed one foot and then another on a new step being birthed. And she rode. She rode the steps of the beast. And this Allister can attest to—she giggled.

Those giggles were the alarm that caught the mother's attention to the lack of child in her maternal glove. Those giggles were what swiveled the mother's body back to the beast. And those giggles were what brought the fear soaring into the mother's eyes, what sent her entire body lurching toward the beast, what brought forth the shriek that some say was heard miles and miles away at another Harrod's Department Store location.

And suddenly, the mother was at the edge of where the steps entered the world, screaming the name of her daughter—which had slipped Allister's memory when he retold this story to me (I will simply refer to her as the girl,but for a more personal and immediate effect, you may feel free to replace 'the girl' with the name of your own daughter).

The Girl still giggled, as she seemed to be ascending into the heavens. The mother paced furiously, franticly. She cursed both Mr. Harrod and Mr. Moving Stair—for, at the time, she did not know the name of Mr. Escalator. And Allister, to the best of his ability, tried to calm her. He insisted that it would be all right, that it was, after all, still Harrod's, that Mr. Harrod would not install a machine in his store that would eat young children. But, the woman was hysterical. She shouted, "What is up there? What is up there?" Though, being a regular at Harrod's, she knew very well that on the second floor was houseware. And, still, the young girl floated. Still, the young girl giggled. A crowd gathered, as crowds do, watched the woman scream, pointed at the young girl rising, and grabbed their hearts with their hands. Someone shouted, "My God!" Then, someone followed with, "Get Mr. Harrod!"

And no one did.

And, as Allister tried to calm the woman, the little girl suddenly caught wind of the tension. She glanced down behind her and saw her mother scream as though she or someone she knew was being murdered. The Girl's giggles immediately turned to tears—an act that could easily be

described as both progressive and regressive maturity. Someone shouted louder, "Get Mr. Harrod!"

And no one did.

The Girl tried to get down to her mother but could not. The steps kept climbing. The Girl screamed. The mother screamed. And the mother broke free from Allister's assistance and leapt to a newly birthed step. Someone shouted still louder, "Get Mr. Harrod!"

And, still, no one did.

The mother—with wobbly, unsure steps—tried to climb up to her daughter, who tried to climb down to her mother. And the escalator held true to its duty (a steady upward motion). The moving steps between them seemed too much and they both sat on a step and sobbed. The crowd gasped, and then, they too, sat and sobbed. Allister stood in awe and confusion at what was happening. Though he, too, eventually had to take a seat. And, from their seats on the immovable ground, they watched as The Girl's step dropped her off at the top ever so simply, ever so lightly.

In the midst of hysterical tears, she was unaware that she had reached the top until her mother, also hysterically unaware, was lightly pushed against her daughter at the second floor. There were cheers from the gathered crowd.

Cheers and sniffles. And the wiping of eyes.

The mother embraced the daughter and would not let go. She held on for dear life until the joy turned to the inevitable spanking—though it could be said that The Girl had not really *disobeyed* at all, that she had merely been curious. Allister watched from below and hoped to himself that the mother would come to her senses, perhaps even reward the courageous explorer with a vase or a spatula from houseware before the two rode the steps down.

And, as the crowd's eyes dried and they dispersed, Allister looked to the escalator and felt sorry for the beast. He could here its pinions, its rotators, whimpering sadly for it knew not what wrong it had done. And Allister, admittedly, knew not what wrong it had done either. So, he simply placed foot to moving step and rode up, knowing that it would take time for the beast to gain back its confidence.
But, the process had to start somewhere.

JOAN OF ARC

llister held one tenet up to all of his lost moments. It was a most simple belief—that one decides whether or not one is lost. And so, Allister (on most occasions) took a breath, and decided that he was not.

On one memorable night, Allister found himself in a courtyard in Orleans. He was young then—perhaps 20. And what brought Allister to this place was somewhat a mystery, though one could not rule out the possibility that the former contents of his empty flask played a large role. In fact, one could not overlook the blaring evidence his empty flask was familiar in many affairs of this sort.

But, Allister would later claim that it was the stars and the moon that beckoned him into the streets of France to walk alone by their guidance. And, when they had led him into unknown alleys and down strange side streets, Allister took that breath and made the decision that he was not lost. He stumble-stepped into the open courtyard and looked to the sky—which was much the same as it had been at the beginning of the night.

He set his hand to rest on some carved stone pedestal to steady himself. The stars and the moon reached down to reveal that resting six feet above Allister was Joan of Arc, on horseback and holding a sword. Allister cocked his head so

simply to the left and looked up. He could feel the whiskey slosh against his cranium. And it could have been the sloshing sensation. It could have been the whiskey itself. Or, it could have been that new place he had found lit by the night. But, Allister found himself climbing the pedestal.

Climbing so that he balanced just in front of the great bronze horse.

And, ever so deliberately, Allister reached for the bronze reins. He felt them in his hand, the coolness of them, how odd that reins could be so frozen, how uncomfortable it must be for Joan and her horse to have been held still for so long. And Allister tugged. Gently at first. Then a little harder, just enough to let the horse know that it was time to move again. And it did. The horse moved its bronze neck, let its bronze head be led by Allister—who guided it from the pedestal to place its hooves on the Earth.

Allister lifted a hand to Joan who had yet to move from her pose. But, at that request, she did. She shook her head to deny Allister the offer and, instead, dismounted with a steadied and casual ease, landing with a light touch of the feet—lighter than you could imagine bronze feet ever landing. Joan looked at Allister and smiled happily. Allister would never forget the smile. For, though the night could be attributed to the delusions of whiskey, the propping of the corners of those bronze lips brought with it a simple warmth that Allister had never felt before or since. Just as Joan, from bronze, became real; Allister felt himself, from whiskey, become sober.

Joan brought her sword to rest on Allister's shoulder. Allister, knowingly, knelt as Joan brought the sword back up and then rested it upon Allister's other shoulder, knighting him. Joan laughed silently and Allister laughed audibly, for they both knew that Joan was only a soldier herself— a two-year veteran at just 19 years old. And there they laughed.

So much had changed since her bronzing. There had been hatred. There had been a canonization. But, she was just 19. Allister was already older than she by perhaps an entire year and, as time would reveal, he would still have many years to come. Were there any questions trapped beneath that bronze?

Joan said nothing, but simply looked up to see the tall buildings, see the simple dirt streets of the city she had saved now paved. Allister instinctually offered Joan his hand again. And, this time, she accepted it. Allister never felt bronze so real.

Together, they explored Orleans for the first time— Allister for his first time at night and Joan for her first time in the twentieth century. From Joan, there was no sound, much laughter, and a slew of firsts: a first glimpse of an automobile, a first ride on a bike (which resulted in a first fall from a bike), a first listen to a trumpet blare sweet jazz, whilst Joan and Allister peeked into her first glimpse of a smoke-filled club, a first dance; a second dance would follow—both would be filled with clumsy human missteps on bronze feet, to Allister's embarrassment.

And before the sun rose, before Allister watched Joan grab her bronze sword and mount her bronze horse, and before Allister guided them back atop the pedestal, Allister gave Joan a simple first kiss. In return, Joan gave Allister her final bronze smile as he fell asleep at her horse's hooves.

And when the sun peeked above the horizon, it found them both in a courtyard in Orleans.

SECRET PASSAGES

ow, Allister always had a fascination for book shelves masquerading as doors and boards in the floor that lifted and revealed a tunnel delving deep below the house, larger in both space and character. If one ever walked into Allister's house, that would be most evident. Perhaps not at first, for that is not the nature of secret passages.

But, notice the barely recognizable oddness in the construction of the cupboard door. Go ahead. Pull it open from the side opposite the handle where the hinges should hold it fast to the base. See that it most certainly opens that way, too. One side reveals grain, the other a passageway to the secret grain in Allister's secret cellar.

Look harder at that light fixture. Pull it down and find that it gives with your weight and the wall moves aside, revealing another room impeccably furnished and arranged in the manner of the room you just left—to the point, of course, that if you look harder at the light fixture in the secret room, if you pull it down, you will find that it also gives with your weight and the wall moves aside, revealing another room impeccably furnished and arranged in the manner of the room you just left—which, of course you will remember, was furnished and arranged in the same manner of that very original room.

There would most certainly be a peculiar light fixture in that room and it would most certainly lead to another room much the same and this could most certainly go on for as long as you are surprised and interested in finding secret identical rooms.

The love of the secret passageways spread and Allister looked to find them in objects (books where secret punctuation on the first page slid aside and revealed the ending in most pure, descriptive form) and people (a widening in the pupil where one could just barely squeeze through, sliding down a passageway that led to various organs—including heart, lungs, and brain—and a greater understanding).

Allister dreamt of a secret passage that would forever hide him from danger and simultaneously get him to wherever he needed to be as soon as he needed to be there. In his dreams this passageway began from almost anywhere— be it sidewalk or loaf of bread. A cement panel in the sidewalk would open; a slice of bread would shift aside and reveal the opening to a grocery store or to China. And, if needed, direct access to a grocery store in China.

That is why one might have found Allister most precisely pulling slices of bread, one at a time, from a loaf and jumping aside afterward. It is also why one might have found Allister attempting to pull on a street lamp or lifting a horse's tongue and reaching underneath it for extra space.

Though one can only guess as to whether he ever found secret passageways in any of his attempts (and, if so, did they remain secret once Allister passed), one could most certainly surmise—as I have—that the possibility remained strong that Allister has not passed away at all. That simply, by way of breath, he shifted the tiniest of air particles aside, revealing a secret passageway into the sky.

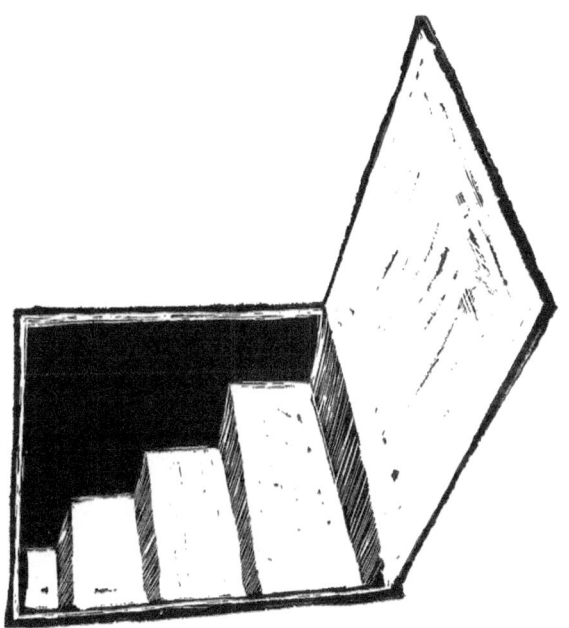

Good night, everyone.
Sleep tight.

FairWeatherBelle.com

www.ingramcontent.com/pod-product-compliance
Lightning Source LLC
Chambersburg PA
CBHW020316150626
46552CB00022B/2900